T0366083

BRIAN DOUGLAS BEVERLY

ONWARD

Order this book online at www.trafford.com
or email orders@trafford.com

Most Trafford titles are also available at major online book retailers.

Printed in the United States of America.

ISBN: 978-1-4669-3280-7 (sc)

Trafford rev. 05/02/2012

 www.trafford.com

North America & international
toll-free: 1 888 232 4444 (USA & Canada)
phone: 250 383 6864 ♦ fax: 812 355 4082

Brian Douglas Beverly

Other books by Brian Douglas Beverly:

HOBO

<u>HOBO II</u>
THE JOURNEY

I'LL BE THERE AT THE TOP OF THE
MOUNTAIN

Brian Douglas Beverly

Acknowledgements

When I was a boy, elderly people told me about the years of the depression when I was around them for some certain reasons. When I cut their grass with the lawn-mower, and the times I was with my grand father. Also, I had an Uncle Hobo, who's name was Clarence Tyler. And he was called Hobo because in the years of the depression he really was one. The stories they'd tell me was very interesting and I liked hearing them. So when I decided to write—HOBO is what I came up with.

Author's Note

Choo Choo Train Clarence Taylor come's to know more of what it is to be a hobo, and get's Rhonda Smalls her moniker. And in part III of HOBO, you'll find there are times when the shacks are hot after them and getting away from the shacks is the biggest challenge.

ONWARD

The Chattanooga Train Station

~1~

Morning has come, and Choo Choo Train Clarence Taylor has Rhonda Smalls stolen aboard a train with him. It's coming into the downtown Chattanooga train station in Tennessee. It's been a long night since they got aboard in Atlanta, Georgia. The train is not slowing down enough before reaching town, so they'll have to move out fast when the train stops, because of the bulls and the shacks. If they see Choo Choo Train and Rhonda Smalls, it'll be trouble for them.

"Listen Rhonda, since we couldn't get off back there on the edge of town, we're really gonna have to break for it. You be sure and move out fast," says Choo Choo Train Clarence Taylor.

"Yeah. but still there's going to be too many people around, maybe in just a little bit we'll be going again, so why don't we try to stay put?" Rhonda asks.

"You know . . . you could be right about that, I can see they'll be taking on more water, and here comes more coal for the burner too, just as we're stopping," says Choo Choo Train.

The both of them are standing off to the side of the big open doorway of the boxcar and have only their faces protruding out to see where the train comes to a halt. The train stops, the railroad crew is getting off and will enter the depot.

"The shacks just went in the depot," says Rhonda.

"Yeah, but look there, those are hired on policemen—that's the bulls," replies Choo Choo Train.

"Let's hope they don't go ta looking us over," says Rhonda.

"We're just gonna have to break for it, that's all," says Choo Choo Train.

He is right; the bulls step down from off the front of the depot and head for the train to look it over. There are five of them armed with black Billy-Clubs. Two of the bulls stop at the first boxcar just after the furnace. Then two climb the ladder to see if there's any hoboes riding up there. One of the bulls keeps walking ahead of them and is looking underneath the train.

"Wait until those two get all the way up there, then we'll jump down and take to that street over there and keep going into town. If they see us, they'll chase after us. But there's a good chance we'll lose 'em in the streets and can hide out until we get on our way again," says Choo Choo Train.

Soon after Choo Choo Train finishes talking, he and Rhonda Smalls jump down from out of the boxcar and run as fast as they can, away

2

from the train. The bull in the lead looking under the train for stole-aways turns around and sees them.

"There's two! Get 'n out a here!" He's pointing in their direction, humped over with eyes staring.

"Yeah, and would ya look at that get'n out. Running faster than ever, too!" shouts one at the top of the boxcar.

"Keep looking it over. We'll get after them," say the two bulls at the first boxcar.

The both of them sprint going in the direction of the two hoboes that just disembarked the train.

Choo Choo Train Clarence Taylor and Rhonda Smalls manage to run out of the train yard and get across a street with buildings on both sides.

"Choo Choo Train! Come this way! Let's cut through here!" Rhonda says excitedly and breathing hard. She waves him over to where she's taking a path from the front to the back of buildings.

"Come on, they went this way!" the bull in the lead shouts at the one behind him. The bulls get from the front to the back of some buildings and stop cold. They've lost sight of Choo Choo Train and Rhonda Smalls.

"The main street is just ahead, so let's get there and see if we can't see 'em," one bull suggests.

Once they've reached the main street where there is some business, the two bulls stand still again, looking in all directions.

"I don't see 'em. Do you?"

"No, I don't see 'em either, and now there's too many people around here. They could have stopped running and blended-in."

"Let's ask a couple of people if they seen 'em runnin' past."

Choo Choo Train and Rhonda Smalls stop running and are walking at a fast pace. They're half a mile away from the bulls and have entered into a neighborhood coming from the downtown area.

"It looks like we lost 'em," says Choo Choo Train.

"Yeah, but let's keep up the pace," Rhonda Smalls answers back to him.

They're looking for some place to go and wait for when the coast is clear, so they can get aboard another train that's headed to Toledo, Ohio. The two bulls have stopped chasing them and made their way back to the depot.

"We lost them boys! They ran where some houses are and got out of sight," says one of the bulls. They have completed their search and didn't find any other hoboes on board. They've all gathered around the two that came back from the chase.

~ 2 ~

Choo Choo Train and Rhonda Smalls are wandering around back streets and staying away from high dollar places. They manage to find a little store on one of the back streets that gets it on like a business route. A beauty salon is next to the little store, and there is a shoe store that sells a lot of boots, as well. Across the street is a Bar. Some of the people around there are standing against the two-story buildings and some of them are sitting on the ground.

Choo Choo Train shows Rhonda the last five dollars he has left over from the money he's had since he left Suffolk, which is his little town in Virginia where he is from.

"Yeah, I see that Choo Choo Train, it's five dollars. You see me? I got my lucky nickel that's been burning a hole in my pocket," says Rhonda Smalls showing the nickel as she opens her palm. He tells her to keep the nickel and come into the store, to see what they can buy to eat with his five dollars.

"Good morning. Is there something I can help you with?" asks the store clerk behind the counter who's also the owner.

"We thought to look around first, but I can see those cans of peaches on the shelf against the wall back there," answers Choo Choo Train.

"Those are 2 for 50 cents cans of peaches," the clerk shouts at him as he goes for the shelf.

"How much are the ginger snaps?" asks Rhonda Smalls.

"Those are 25 cents for 3 pounds," the clerk answers.

"Choo Choo Train, do you want to get the ginger snaps too?"

"No," answers Choo Choo Train. Choo Choo Train pays for the peaches and then he and Rhonda go back outside.

"I'm looking at that Bar over there across the street," he says taking the can of peaches away from his mouth.

"Why? Are you gonna get drunk?" ask Rhonda.

"Kind of. Come on."

They go to the Bar, and once inside, they find the crowded smoke-filled room is very noisy. Choo Choo Train makes his way over to a man who's standing near the bar, and Rhonda stays back by the door.

"Say, I tell ya what, let's you and me make a bet,' says Choo Choo Train.

"Bet what?"

"That I can drink three mugs of beer, before you can drink three shots."

"Ole no, you can't."

Brian Douglas Beverly

"Let's get closer to the bar. Now here's the bet: I'll set my mugs up here in front of me, and you put three shots of Whiskey there at you, for 50 cent plus who pays for the drinks."

The crowd quiets down, and the man tells him the bet's on. Some were sitting, but now they're standing nearby, watching Choo Choo and the man. The ones already standing have gathered around and move in closer.

"The rules are. you can't touch my mugs no matter what. And I can't touch your shot glasses no matter what. And you start getting your shots after I set my first mug down," Choo Choo Train explains.

"That sounds good to me, partner. And you make good and for sure not to knock my Whiskey shots off the Bar that you said there's no touch 'n 'em—you'll see how fast I can drink 'em before you ever drink them mugs of beer."

Choo Choo Train grabs on to one of his mugs and looks into the man's eyes.

"I'm ready," he says taking the mug from off the top of the bar and does not stop drinking until the last drop of beer is gone.

Rhonda can't see over the top of the crowd, so she gets a chair to stand on. She isn't very confident about Choo Choo placing a bet like this. Her eyes are partly closed. She's squinting at the event, looking worried.

"Now there," says Choo Choo Train, and turns the empty beer mug over, setting it upside down over the top of one of the shot glasses so the

7

shot is trapped under the mug. Now the man can't get to it without moving Choo Choo Train's beer mug.

"Oh," Rhonda gasps and now has a look of surprise on her face.

"Y... that's unfair! We're not supposed to touch 'em!" The man shouts.

"I ain't touch'n it. But you can't get to it unless you touch mine. Can ya?"

"I didn't know you was gonna do it like that, I thought you was gonna try and drink 'em faster than me."

"Yeah, that's it, see! I can take all of the time I need to, and if you pick my mug up to get to your shot of whisky, then you touched it, and that means you're disqualified. So you may as well give the 50 cents here."

"I believe to kick your ass instead of giving you the 50 cents on that."

"No, you see, I win the bet then." The man moves in closer to Choo Choo Train and punches him in the mouth. Choo Choo Train falls backwards, and is quick to his feet, ready to fight back. The man throws another punch, hitting Choo Choo Train on the side of his head. Choo Choo Train punches the man hard in the belly after that blow to his head. As the man bends over, Choo Choo Train hits him with an upper cut to the chin, knocking the man out cold.

"Ok, you back off now!" shouts the bartender aloud through the crowd at Choo Choo Train Clarence Taylor.

"Say Mister, why don't you go outside and we'll get your winnings for ya?" says one of the others standing there.

Going for the door, Choo Choo sees Rhonda getting down off the chair and makes his way over to where she is.

"Hurry Choo Choo Train," she says waving him over.

"I'm come'n."

Outside the Bar, they've landed just a few feet away from the door, and standing in the dirt, that has patches of grass through it—there isn't a sidewalk.

"Ole boy! They said they're gonna bring you the money!"

"That's if he's got it. I'm thinkin' he just knew he could beat out on my mugs by drinkin' his shots faster. So he went on ahead and betted. And there's not gonna be no money what so ever to his name, and that's how's come he took a swing at me, too."

"Ole no... that's right, it could be. Look, a couple of them are coming our way."

"Say partner, me and Otis here was wonderin'. Seein's how things done come about. Can we have the two mugs of beer you left on the bar?"

Just then a crowd of men bursts the door open and spills out of the Bar. They stand in front of Choo Choo Train and Rhonda Smalls.

"He finally snapped out of it," one reports.

"Yeah, and we didn't think he would," another man says who's standing there and gets them laughing.

"Anyways, here's the 50 cents from Judson. That's ole Judson Voideman in there. When he came to, he just coughed it right up." Choo Choo Train takes the money from the man and tells the two gents they can have the mugs of beer left on the bar. As they all go back inside, he turns to Rhonda.

"Come on Rhonda, let's you and me go back to the store and get them ginger snaps. Here's one of the quarters to go with that nickel."

"Ole boy! Thanks, Choo Choo Train."

Brian Douglas Beverly

~ 3 ~

In Suffolk Virginia, Barbo Brown is at the depot unloading a train that came in a day before. Barbo Brown had gone for Haddy, Jane, and Mary when Choo Choo Train was born. They were the three midwives, and Barbo had been a part of them since the beginning of their time in Suffolk. He now is an elderly man and can handle lifting only so much of the cargo.

"I'm taking a break, I'll be right back," says Barbo.

He walks away from the boxcar and goes into the depot where a log's burning in the fireplace. He sits in a chair nearby with others already gathered around.

"Say... Barbo, it's good you came in," says the telegraph operator.

"There ain't been nothin' coming over the wire, so I felt to sit here awhile," he finishes.

"Them young men are get'n hard to keep up with, so I gotta take a break," says Barbo.

Brian Douglas Beverly

"Mr. Foster may be gettin' that contract with Jacksonville Florida. We'll be back 'n forth with 'em, so you best get prepared."

"I will be, especially because that's gonna be steady work."

"Yes, and we'll be takin' on some other workers, too. And during these times here, that'll be very good," adds the telegraph operator.

Here in 1932 at the Seaboard Air Lines Railways in Suffolk, Virginia, trains don't come in with passengers as often as they used to. The Stock Market Crash offset businesses throughout the country, that even the locomotives are affected by it. Moreover, people can no longer pay for passenger trains and have them riding the rails, as expected.

Barbo goes back to work and finishes unloading the cargo in two more hours. Then he goes to Joe and Betty's Kitchen-in.

"I'm buying, since we had a train come in loaded down with cargo and it paid us workers as good as it did," says Barbo Brown.

"Thank you Barbo, if you can afford to pay, I'll take you up on it," Sally replies.

"I may be out at the sawmill next week, and from then on," says Nate who's married to Choo Choo Train's mother Sally.

The three midwives are there, as well.

"Have you heard from Clarence these past few days? Because I sure could have used his help like we used to do," Barbo asks Sally.

"No, but he was gettin' a train out'a Florida for Toledo, Ohio, the last time I talked to him. He's dead-set on getting' work up there," Sally finishes.

ONWARD

"The next time Clarence calls you, tell him that Mr. Foster is in good communications with Jacksonville, Florida, and it looks like there's gonna be a contract to do trains' movements back and forth with them. And if it do, then Clarence can come back to his job at the depot."

All of them sitting at the table are in good spirits about Barbo's news. And for dinner, they order the special posted on a sign daily at the front entrance of the kitchen-in.

14

~4~

Choo Choo Train and Rhonda Smalls are walking through the woods on the outskirts of town. His bundle is fixed up on a long stick from off the Georgia pine. And Rhonda is calling up to him from behind.

"Choo Choo Train, don't you think we're gonna be too far off to catch a train out here?"

"I never thought we walked that much away from where the depot's at."

"Yes we did, and it's too far, because the train's gonna be movin' out too fast to hop it. As soon as we get out'a this Tennessee hickory and to them railroad tracks that's out this way, you'll see."

"Yeah... I think you're right," Choo Choo says, as he looks around. He thinks to himself, the sun is going down and it's gonna get too dark to see.

"Good, we're out of the woods," Rhonda sounds off, joyous and in good spirits.

"There's the tracks in front of us—up the hill where the man at the store said they'd be when we got the ginger snaps," says Choo Choo Train.

They're walking into the clear, where there's enough sunlight to see. Tennessee is still cold at dusk in the springtime of the year.

"We're almost through this field. Then we can walk up the little hill the tracks are on," says Choo Choo Train.

"That's right," agrees Rhonda.

They've reached the railroad tracks and go in the direction of the train station.

"We're gettin' the wind up here Choo Choo Train, and it's cold."

"I know it, I feel it too."

"It's gonna be too dark by the time we reach the train yard," says Rhonda.

"Let's get closer, then we'll get back in the trees and I'll light us a fire," says Choo Choo Train.

Rhonda Smalls has no trouble keeping up with him. She's able to walk fast on the railroad ties. Choo Choo Train is walking as though he's in a trance. He is thinking of home, and mixes his thoughts with what he wants to happen for him in Toledo, Ohio. He is imagining that everyone he knows in Tidewater is proud of the job he got established at a factory, and they're all making plans to come see him there. And in Toledo, Choo Choo Train Clarence Taylor dreams he's found a nice house in a nice neighborhood and knows his neighbors.

16

"You know, I think I love you now Choo Choo Train. You manage to get the ginger snaps and plus you gave me one of the quarters," he hears Rhonda saying.

Her voice takes him by surprise. He turns quickly to look in her direction and keeps walking forward, then turns back—looking ahead.

"Oh what were you thinkin' about? I didn't know you were lost in thought."

"Nothing, when we get back to the train yard I'm gonna try to reach home."

"Oh, so that's what you were thinkin' about?"

Choo Choo Train doesn't say anything more, and keeps walking.

~5~

Darkness overtakes them now, so they go back into the woods and find a place to bed down.

"We'll fix-up here," says Choo Choo Train.

"Ok, I can still see where the tracks are through the trees the way we came back in the woods," Rhonda talks paranoid – he can tell from the sound of her voice.

"Yeah, we just came in through there. The moon's got the field lit up that you can still see," says Choo Choo Train.

"It's a full moon," Rhonda replies.

"I'll be sure and not tell you any spooky stories about the full moon," says Choo Choo Train.

"What spooky stories?"

"It's when the Werewolves start howling and ghosts come out, on a full moon night."

"That's right; don't tell me at a time like this."

They gather up firewood from where they are standing, and Choo Choo Train takes some matches from his coat pocket and lights the fire. Then they open their satchels and lay open on the ground the cloth their satchels are fixed into, on opposite sides of the campfire. They place themselves on top of the spread, on their backs with their hands locked behind their heads.

"How's about them ginger snaps?" he asks.

Rhonda tosses him the bag; he catches it with both hands and gets a handful of cookies, then tosses them back over to where she is.

"You were thinking a lot when we were walking on the tracks. You wish you were back home, don't you?" asks Rhonda.

"It don't matter now, because we're well on our way to Toledo. It's too late to go back," Choo Choo Train answers.

"That's right."

"But I intend to check-up on things at the train station tomorrow."

"We can't go too close to the depot, the bulls will still be there, and they'll see us. I need to call Atlanta and tell my people there that I left, so we're just gonna have to figure out something."

"Yeah,.. that's right, I forgot about that."

"We'll just have to wait until later."

Choo Choo Train is quiet now, eating his fist fill of ginger snaps and looking into the fire—thinking.

"What's it like in your town?" Rhonda asks.

"Ole... it's quiet, most of the time. We go after game when it's winter.

ONWARD

I shot one deer in my life—a few rabbits and some pheasants from out of a cornfield. But I did very little trapping for pelts. I was working at the depot when all this for me came about. And we sang songs too," Choo Choo Train finishes.

"I see, we'd sing at the Church, I used to be in the Choir," says Rhonda.

"Oh… Yeah… that's right. There were times we'd sing around by the depot."

"What kind of songs did you sing?"

"We'd make 'em up, mostly. And mostly it was folk songs."

He eats the last ginger snap in his hand and rolls over, getting off the big cloth. He stands on his feet, turns sideways away from Rhonda Smalls.

"Here's a song I'd sing every now and then," Choo Choo says.

"*Birds are flying high flap flap your wings fly high birds and you know your skies when you are traveling no matter where you fly—birds are flying high flap flap birds.*"

Rhonda rises up from off her back and is sitting up laughing at his singing. Choo Choo Train is leaning to one side looking up at the tops of trees to see the sky. He has one elbow sticking out, and he's moving it back and forth like a bird's wings flapping. And he hops, switching from one foot to the other.

"You see there Rhonda Smalls, we'd have the best time going on and get ta feeling fine," he says.

20

Brian Douglas Beverly

She sits smiling and not saying anything. Choo Choo Train puts another log on the fire. The both of them lie back down and fall asleep. The fire rises to a brilliant burning flame and has it warm all about them as they lie there in the peace and quiet of the Forest.

21

ONWARD

~6~

It's the next day, and at the Chattanooga Choo Choo Train Station, the railroad crew is working diligently to get the train going on its way. Some of the passengers are getting aboard, and there are two boxcars connected to the passenger cars of the Chattanooga Choo Choo. The Cincinnati Southern railways had their first train get to Chattanooga railways in 1880, to establish north to south transporting by way of a train, which started the Chattanooga Choo Choo.

"Don't look now, but here comes smart Cowcatcher Bruce Young," says Flats Rubin Bar.

There are four hoboes sitting around a campfire near the Chattanooga train station with coffee brewing. And one other just walks into camp, who's called Cowcatcher Bruce Young.

"Whatta ya know good boys?" asks Cowcatcher Bruce Young.

"We thought ta ask you, as for us you see it," answers Flats Rubin Bar.

"I'll be headed out on the noon train to Cincinnati, Ohio. I smelled the coffee and thought I'd come and get some of it," says Cowcatcher Bruce Young.

He's called Cowcatcher because he rides on the pointed metal skirt mounted on the front of the engine. At times, he's called smart because he wears six shirts under his coat and five pairs of pants to protect him from rocks and any other debris when he's riding the rails. He also puts on a hat stuffed with socks.

"You bet you get your coffee, you're the top hobo riding the cowcatcher," says Flats.

"You been knocked unconscious yet?" says one of the other hoboes who's sitting there.

"No, he couldn't have been, he'd be dead from slippin' off," answers Flats.

Flats Rubin Bar got his moniker because he gets claustrophobic riding in boxcars. He also has fear of heights and can't ride on top of the boxcars, so he can only steal aboard flat bed railroad train cars.

"A deer came across the tracks once, and it almost was hit by the cowcatcher with me on it," says Cowcatcher.

"You got your cup?" Another hobo asks Cowcatcher Bruce Young as he goes for the coffee pot for himself.

"Yep, I got it right here." He gets in his satchel and brings out a tin cup. He plans to spend the rest of the morning there with them by the fire.

~ 7 ~

Choo Choo Train Clarence Taylor and Rhonda Smalls have awakened; they've fixed up their satchels to make way for the new day.

"The fire's still burnin'," says Rhonda.

"I'll throw some dirt on it and smother it out," says Choo Choo Train.

After he puts out the fire, they walk out of the woods and across the field.

"It didn't seem like we were this far away last night," says Rhonda as she's walking up the hill to get to the train tracks.

"It didn't seem like it to me, either."

"We're gonna be too tired to hop a train by the time we get there," says Rhonda. "We might be able to sit a spell."

"How do you know if a train's leaving today or not?"

"It looked busy enough last night."

They're walking in the opposite direction of the sun rising and their footsteps tromping down with boonedocker boot shoes on their feet is

24

like a bunch of people coming past. And they've got the long sticks hung over their shoulders with a bundle tied at the end of it. The tracks round in from out of the outer banks, then go straight again—headed into town.

"I can see the train yard from here," says Rhonda.

"I can, too. We've picked up on some more railroad tracks leading to the train station," says Choo Choo Train.

"It smells like something's burning," Rhonda says looking in all directions and sniffing in the air.

"There's a fire over there," says Choo Choo Train pointing at the fire.

"Look at them with that campfire Choo Choo Train, they're doing like us. Maybe we can go over to 'em and find out something," she finishes.

"Yeah, let's go over and see, that'll be good if they let us sit a spell and get some of that coffee."

"Saayy . . . wait a minute. When we get to 'em I want you to call me Mr. Smalls. That way they won't know I'm a lady. You can't hardly tell by looking at me can ya?"

"You spoof 'n me?"

"No, I'm not spoof 'n, I mean it."

They walk down the hill from off the tracks and go over to where the hoboes are gathered around the fire.

"It looks like them two's comin' our way," says Flats Rubin Bar.

"Do any of you know 'em?" asks Cowcatcher Bruce Young.

The other hoboes shake their heads saying no, and watch them on the approach.

"Sure, you two can come here with your satchels and rest awhile," says one of the hoboes.

"You got a name?" asks one of the others sitting there.

"This here is Choo Choo Train Clarence Taylor, and I'm Mr. Smalls. We come in from Atlanta, Georgia on the morning train yesterday."

"I never heard of any a' you," says Flats Rubin.

"That's right," Cowcatcher Bruce chimes in.

"How's about some of that coffee?" Choo Choo Train is pointing at the pot placed on the fire as he and Rhonda sit down.

One of the hoboes picks it up and is ready to pour the coffee. They get their tin cups from out of their satchels and have the coffee black.

"I left Tidewater Virginia some days ago, now. I hopped a train there first bound for Ohio," says Choo Choo Train.

"Whereabouts in Ohio?" asks Flats Rubin.

"It was going to Cincinnati, then I was gonna pay a passenger train from there to Toledo," answers Choo Choo Train.

"What happened?" Cowcatcher Bruce asks.

"The train I was on went to Jacksonville, Florida instead. So I picked oranges at an orange grove in Naples and came this far from there."

"There's a noon train leaving for Cincinnati today. It's the Chattanooga Choo Choo, I'll be getting' aboard it," says Cowcatcher

Bruce Young.

"That's right! And ya know what?! I'll tell you two right now. That, this here is smart Cowcatcher Bruce Young that you're talking to," Flats Rubin Bar shouts excitedly.

"You see. . . he gets aboard riding the cowcatcher!" Flats Rubin continues.

"And he's smart Cowcatcher, because he wears a bunch of clothes so the debris won't hurt 'em," finishes Flats Rubin Bar.

"That's right; now tell me how did you get your name?" Cowcatcher Bruce asks.

"It was Ride 'em Jack Cuttings," answers Choo Choo Train.

"Ride 'em Jack! You mean the Ride 'em Jack that can steal aboard without being seen in broad daylight at the Philadelphia Pennsylvania yard?!" Flats Rubin sitting cramped on a log leaning forward as though he were reaching out to Choo Choo Train, asks excitedly and wants to hear more about Ride 'em Jack Cuttings.

"We met-up in Tampa and hopped a log roller." Choo Choo Train tells them the rest of when he was with Ride 'em Jack.

A fresh pot of coffee is finish brewing, and they fill their cups again. Rhonda Smalls is very much calmed down now because she's already hopped aboard a train since she's

been out with Choo Choo Train and now is in the company of others-onward. The hoboes can see that Rhonda is with Choo Choo Train and going in his direction.

"It's getin' time for the nooner to disembark, if 'n you two are hoppin' aboard you best be gettin' like me now," says Cowcatcher Bruce Young.

"We're coming," says Choo Choo Train Clarence Taylor.

~8~

Keeping out of sight, they go further into the train yard to get closer to the train, so that it'll be going slow enough for them.

"There she's steaming and ready to go. That's the Cattanooga Choo Choo, and she's bound for Cincinnati, too," says Cowcatcher Bruce. "You two are in a good position right here to get aboard that open boxcar on the end before the caboose," he continues. "You can see it'll be close to only take a few steps when you running ta get into it real fast, before they see ya. Right now, I'll keep low and go for the cowcatcher, it's ta get in front of it before she's movin' out so I can get on," finishes Cowcatcher Bruce Young.

Without any hesitation, he is upon the tracks bent over frontward's and running for the tip of the train.

"He made it, Choo Choo Train, he's on the cowcatcher," says Rhonda Smalls talking just above a whisper.

"Yeah...I see 'em and that's crazy to me riding that way."

"What da ya think, that this is easier than Atlanta?"

"Well … it will be, if the ones in the caboose don't see us. But you can see the open boxcar is hooked up to it."

The Chattanooga Choo Choo gets on its way and just when it comes rolling past; they run to the open boxcar and leap inside. The both of them move to the back wall and sit down on the floor. From out of the front comes the front brakeman and has his brake club in his hand. The club is a stout stick used to increase leverage in setting hand breaks on railroad cars. The front brakeman saw Choo Choo Train and Rhonda Smalls get aboard. He gets to the open door of the boxcar and throws himself in.

"Hay there, you two!" he shouts rising up from off his hands and knees.

"Oh no! One of the shacks is get 'n in!" cries Rhonda Smalls.

Choo Choo Train immediately thrusts himself off the floor and into the shack before the man can swing his brake club. Gripping his arms tightly around the shack midways at his body, Choo Choo Train brings him down. When they land on the floor of the boxcar, the shack's head is sticking out of the boxcar with Choo Choo Train on top of him. The shack can see the sky and the trees behind him upside down sweeping past at a fast pace, and the force of the wind is pressing against his head. Choo Choo Train Clarence Taylor hits him in the nose with his fist.

"I'm Hewey Pewitt!" cries the shack as he throws his brake club into

30

the open air.

"Choo Choo Train, get up! Get off of 'em!" shouts Rhonda Smalls. With the back of Choo Choo's coat gripped tight in her fist, she's pulling at him with all her might. She manages to drag Choo Choo Train away from Hewey Pewitt, and they both throw themselves on the floor. Hewey Pewitt gets up. Now standing tall in the boxcar, he is very scared and talks about himself.

"I'm not really one of the Wichita linemen that's out of Wichita, I just only told 'em that, so they'd take me on and I can have something to eat and have some place to go. I can't really fight nobody, go ahead, sit down. I don't know why they don't let anybody climb aboard that wants to. Is it bleeding?" he asks touching his nose as he sits down with Rhonda Smalls and Choo Choo Train.

"A little bit," Rhonda answers.

"Are you a woman?" Hewey asks.

"That's right," answers Choo Choo Train.

"I guess you can tell that with my hat off," says Rhonda as she picks her hat up off the floor and puts it back on her head.

"We've only been back and forth from Kentucky to Tennessee, and we hardly picked up any cargo because of what's hittin'. They're calling this here—Years of the depression," finishes Hewey Pewitt.

The locomotive has reached top speed, and the three of them have gotten comfortable in the boxcar. They're in good communications with each other. Choo Choo Train and Rhonda Smalls are very confident about making their goal, and it shows. Hewey Pewitt sees them differently, other than like desperate bums or tramps and even other than like hoboes. Their correspondence to him is as though two companions are in good communications with their neighbor.

"You were saying that you only been back and forth to Kentucky and Tennessee? Well... Now... How is that? Because this here is the Chattanooga, and it goes to Cincinnati where we're headed," says Choo Choo Train.

"It's these two boxcars, they're from Lexington, Kentucky where me and them is get'n off at. The train will continue on with the passengers from there. The boxcar ahead of us has some cargo; but as you can see, there's nothin' in this one. They're gonna be switchin' tracks for us, though. You see, our people can reach 'em down there, in Florida. And not have the cargo train go to Chattanooga on these times comin'. Because they explain to them that the Chattanooga people won't let the produce come through. And this time of the year, we just plowed our fields for planting. We still have to have our crops happen for us."

After Hewey Pewitt explains the train movement to them, Choo Choo Train and Rhonda Smalls talk more about their onward journey.

"I'm going to live with my Aunt and Uncle that's in Toledo. I already made arrangements with them, they said for me to get there and I can have some space in their house," says Rhonda Smalls.

"You're lucky to have that ahead of you Rhonda," says Choo Choo

Train.

"Yes, and she was lucky hopping in this boxcar too, because she's a woman. I saw when you two stole aboard and she barely got her leg up. But I thought it was some little guy," says Hewey Pewitt.

"That's right about you being lucky too, Rhonda, just like get'n aboard in Atlanta. I'm going to Toledo to work in a factory and get me a house good in a neighborhood," explains Choo Choo Train.

They all become silent the rest of the way to Oneida, where the Tran will be taking on water.

"We must be hittin' Oneida, its slowing down like it is," says Choo Choo Train.

"I'll take a look," says Hewey Pewitt.

He goes to the door and looks past the engine to see the water tower and depot growing closer and closer. Just when he's looking, Cowcatcher Bruce Young hops off the cowcatcher and runs away from the train.

"Oh no," shouts Hewey Pewitt.

"What is it?" Rhonda asks.

"I just saw a hobo jump off the cowcatcher."

"That's Cowcatcher Bruce Young. He ain't too scared to ride up there," says Choo Choo Train.

"Yeah, but that's too dangerous and foolish. That's why there's a penalty for it, or we'll chase you away. There's deaths at that all the time," finishes Hewey Pewitt.

ONWARD

The train stops completely, and Hewey explains to them they can stay put and he'll have it covered with the rest of the shacks.

~9~

"What happened to you, Hewey? I had to engage the breaks up front and where's that brakeman's club?" asks the fireman.

"I thought I saw somethin' back at the boxcars and when I went to look, the train was moving, so I ended up staying back there," Hewey answers.

"Well... What did ya see?"

"It was nothing."

A lot of the passengers going to Cincinnati take time to disembark the train and walk around.

"Yeah... He got it covered for us," says Choo Choo Train.

"That's good, but I need to pee," says Rhonda.

"No one's paying attention, so we can get down and go behind the water tower," says Choo Choo Train.

The train station is so crowded, nobody sees them climb off the boxcar and walk about the station.

"I'm gonna go behind these trees here, I'll be right back," says Rhonda.

Choo Choo Train watches the steamer quickly fill up with water. Not long after, Rhonda gets back. They watch the spout get put away and then they walk away from the water tower.

"Wait Rhonda, something occured to me," says Choo Choo Train.

"What?"

"You need to have your name carved here."

"What do you mean, Choo Choo Train?"

"Like me. Let's climb up the water tower and figure out put'n our monikers."

They get themselves situated up on the ladder leaning against the water tower.

"Now here's me," says Choo Choo as he takes out his pocketknife, and begins to carve "Choo Choo Train Clarence Taylor" in the wood. "You see there, Rhonda Smalls?" he says proudly, when he finishes.

"Yeah, I see. And look at all of these other hobo names. I don't know what to call myself," says Rhonda.

"You have to think of a special name," says Choo Choo.

"How about, Hobo Woman Rhonda Smalls Aboard? Or Get'n Aboard Rhonda?" says Rhonda Smalls.

"Nah, that's not catchy enough. It needs to go along with ya, somethin' about yourself, and the way you are. I notice that you're lucky, and that shack, Hewey Pewitt pointed that out. That'll be it,

Lucky Rhonda Smalls Riding the Rails. No...Wait a minute! Lucky Rails Rhonda Smalls."

"That's it, Choo Choo Train!" shouts Rhonda with excitement.

He gives Lucky Rails Rhonda his pocketknife so she can carve her moniker on the water tower.

"That's it, put yours next to mine. And let's get back on the train while no one's lookin'."

Hewey Pewitt talks to the rest of the railroad crew about Cowcatcher Bruce Young, and tells them to watch and see if he tries to get back on the cowcatcher. The passengers are all aboard once again. The train is slowly getting on its way, and just as the first whistle's blowing and the wheels grind slowly on top of the iron rails, comes Cowcatcher Bruce Young. Immediately, two shacks that stayed behind to work at the depot come for him.

"Look, Choo Choo Train! There's the Cowcatcher, and he's gonna get caught!" says Lucky Rails Rhonda sadly.

"I see 'em"

The both of them can see out of the door of the boxcar the two shacks chasing after Cowcatcher, and the train is still moving slow enough that Cowcatcher runs past the cowcatcher and sprints across the tracks in front of it, to get to the other side.

"Did you see that?! He didn't get on! He ran past it!"

Lucky Rails shouts excitedly, but not loud enough to hear over the rumbling of the train.

"So are the shacks, they're close to 'em too, and they probably will catch 'em because he can't run very fast with all of them clothes on," says Choo Choo Train.

Cowcatcher Bruce manages to run fast enough to clear the tracks and into an open field that has the in-coming season's new green grass growing here in the spring. And that's where he is caught. The two shacks rustle Cowcatcher Bruce Young to the ground and take hold of both his arms, dragging him back to the depot for the dispatcher to notify the deputies. Choo Choo Train and Lucky Rails Rhonda can no longer see them because they're on the opposite side of the tracks and the train has gotten far away from the depot now.

~ 10 ~

The train ride to Lexington, Kentucky is without any excitement.

"Hewey Pewitt said these two boxcars are staying in Lexington. I don't see how we can hop the passenger cars," says Lucky Rails.

"I know it, I'm still trying to figure that out," says Choo Choo Train.

They're down on the floor of the boxcar partly asleep and not talking. The seemingly long time riding on the train finally ends. They're pulling into the train yard and the slowing down of the train with breaks applied causes them to rise to their feet. Lucky Rails goes to the door and looks outside.

"It's dark out now, Choo Choo Train."

"I can see it."

"We're gonna have to jump off the train in the dark," she says looking back at Choo Choo Train.

"Hay, you there! I see that you've stolen aboard!" One of the bulls sees Lucky Rails standing in the doorway of the boxcar talking to Choo

ONWARD

Choo Train, and brings a long barrel pistol from out of his belt. With the gun held high, he runs alongside the train and almost catches up to them.

Lucky Rails moves back and presses herself against the wall. Now the train has moved into the light of the globes at the depot and stops.

"That ain't no Hewey Pewitt out there," she says looking up at him.

"That's right."

"Wait a minute, these two boards are broke loose," says Lucky Rails pulling away from the wall.

"All right, don't you move!" The hired policeman sticks the barrel of the gun in.

"So there's two 'a ya?!" he shouts when he sees Choo Choo Train as well.

The both of them can only stand still staring at the bull.

"Get your hands up! That's good! Don't you two move either and stay put!" He closes the door and sees the other bulls and the passengers getting off the train.

"Say, Billy! You and Tom come here!" he shouts with the pistol held in his hand aimed at the door. The two bulls are coming as fast as they can, pressing through the crowd.

"Let me see those loose boards," says Choo Choo Train. He and Lucky Rails put their hands down and crawl over to the spot.

"These are it, Choo Choo Train."

Choo Choo takes both hands and pushes on them.

40

"I got them off at the bottom, and that's a big enough opening for us to get out, too. You go first, Lucky Rails, and hurry-up."

Choo Choo Train is able to free the boards completely from the loose nails down by his feet and swing them to one side. After Lucky Rails jumps down out of the boxcar and onto the ground, he hands her down the two satchels. She props them up against the boxcar and grips the boards for Choo Choo Train so he can slip through. Once he is off, he puts the boards back into position. She hands him his satchel, and the both of them take off running away from the train on the opposite side of the bulls.

"What is it Ralf? You got train hoppers inside?"

"That's right, Tom. Billy, you stand here with me. That's good the two of you have your clubs, they may spring out at me and if I miss, Tom, you open the door."

The bull pushes the door open and all of them can see inside that there's no one there.

"Well...now...just where are they?" asks Billy.

"They're gone," Ralf replies, as he's looking from left to right, then straight ahead.

"Wait a minute. They couldn't have got out of there. Are you sure you seen 'em Ralf?" Tom asks.

"Wait a minute, let me climb in and take a closer look, maybe they're hiding in the shadows," Ralf says.

Ralf gets himself into the boxcar with the pistol still in his hand. He turns left and walks the length of the boxcar. Then he turns to the right and gets to the far wall from the door, and he's stepping off paces looking from top to bottom at the far wall.

"I'm tellin' ya, they ain't here Ralf," Billy replies.

"Just you hang on, I know what I saw. Wait a minute, here's a couple of loose boards."

Ralf punches with his hand to see the boards move, and then gives them a swift kick, breaking them off the one nail that was still holding them.

"Now you see there, boys! They got out through here. I told ya I seen 'em!"

"I believe ya now Ralf," says Tom.

"They're gonna be long gone by now," says Billy.

"There's too many boxcars that needs fix 'n. They need to get better in the roundhouses," Ralf finishes.

~ 11 ~

Choo Choo Train and Lucky Rails keep running straight ahead and go more into the town of Lexington, Kentucky. The air is cool and brisk. In the dark, they can hardly see where they are and don't know their way around town. This time, they'll stay in the downtown area and look for a telephone booth.

"Let's go this way Choo Choo Train, they didn't see us get out back there, so they don't know which way to look," says Lucky Rails.

"That's right. There's got to be a telephone booth around here, somewhere."

"Let's cross the street and look over there."

They allow for some traffic to pass by, and run quickly across to the other side. Lucky Rails is fast walking ahead of Choo Choo Train. She is very eager to talk with her mother in Atlanta, Georgia.

"You see, there's a telephone booth there on the corner. I'll make my call first," she says picking up her pace.

"Never mind me none Lucky Rails, you talk as long as they let ya," says Choo Choo Train as she enters the telephone booth.

"Yes operator, I'd like to reverse the charges."

Excitement builds up in her when the operator makes the connection on the switchboard.

"Hi mom," Lucky Rails yells into the phone, "It's me, Rhonda!"

"How long have you been in Kentucky?"

"Just got here, now."

"I talked to Uncle Chester and Aunt Lizzy last night. They want to know where you are—now I can tell them," says her mom.

"That's right mom, there's been a derailment somewhere that's got the train held up, so I can't leave right now. I'll let you know when we'll take off."

"Alright. Have you been eating?"

"Yes, you don't have to worry. I gotta run now mom, but I'll call again soon."

"Ok, darlin'," her mother says. "Take care of yourself."

"I will mom, I love you," says Lucky Rails, her voice trembling.

She finishes talking with her mother and hangs up the phone. As she steps out of the telephone booth, she gestures to Choo Choo Train standing there. She walks away some distance from him because she is feeling weepy, having just talked to her mother. She makes her way over to a streetlight and reaches the light pole. She leans on the pole with one hand and rests her other hand on her hip. She stares at the cement sidewalk and can't stop sobbing, as she sways her head from side to side.

It's Choo Choo Train's turn on the telephone.

"Yes operator, please dispatch the call through," says Gretchen.

"Hello, Gretchen?"

"Yes Clarence, the operator said its Kentucky, I thought you was headed to Toledo, Ohio?"

"I still am, there's been a delay of the train for some reason. I have to find out. Would you mind get'n mom for me so I can talk to her?"

"She's got her own phone over there, now. Nate works three or five days a week at the sawmill, and they're doing all right with that."

"Good, that's good," Gretchen tells him his mom's telephone number, and they hang up. Meanwhile, Lucky Rails stops crying and comes over to where he is to see how much longer he'll be.

"You almost finished talking?"

"No, I have to call again. That was my neighbor. My mom has a phone at the house now, so I'm calling there."

He dials the operator and gets the call dispatched through.

"Hello Clarence, it's about time you called back," says his mother.

"Right mom, you can tell from the operator I'm here in Kentucky?"

"Yes, how long have you been there?"

"Since today, I'm still going to Toledo. There's been a delay of the train."

"I see. How long before you get going again?"

45

"Tomorrow morning, hopefully."

"I see—if you don't make it out of there, give me a call back."

"Yeah...I will, mom."

"Listen Clarence, Barbo was telling me something about a contract Mr. Foster may be getting with Florida."

"Ole yeah, what's that?"

"He said the Seaboard may contract out to go back and forth to Jacksonville for cargo and if the deal goes through, you can have your job back at the depot and you can come back home."

"That sounds great mom, I'd like to be home if I can work."

"Get me a mailing address as soon as you get there, so I can mail you a letter to let you know, because if you keep calling on the telephone it'll cost too much."

"Wait a minute mom; I might have an address for ya now." He opens the door and speaks to Lucky Rails. "Say, Lucky Rails!"

"What, Choo Choo Train?"

"My mom needs to send me a letter and I was wonderin' if we could give her your Aunt's address."

She gives him the address to her Aunt and Uncle's house for his mother to use, and Clarence says goodbye to his mother and hangs up.

~12~

The both of them walk the streets some more. They're trying to figure out where to go for food and shelter.

"It looked like you were cryin' back there," says Choo Choo Train.

"I'm just getting homesick, that's all. Plus my mother and me have always been close."

"That's the same here, I want to get back home and get my old job back at the depot. I made up a story and told them back home the train is delayed for something is how's come I'm in Kentucky and not Toledo," says Choo Choo Train.

"That's what I did when my mother asked about me, I said there was a derailment."

Choo Choo Train sees a group of people going through the open door of a Church. He leads Lucky Rails to it and finds a soup kitchen.

"Well... What da ya know, Lucky Rails, it's a soup kitchen!"

"Yeah, that's good. I can eat the whole pot too, as long as it ain't

47

beans."

"Say... You two are hoboes drifting' in ain't ya?" a man asks who's in line alongside of them.

"We just only need to take the train," Lucky Rails answers.

"Sure. You've stolen aboard. Do you want to know where there's a jungle?"

"Sure... That'll be good," Choo Choo Train replies.

"There's one west of here. You go back out the door and make a left when you go and keep straight for three miles. You can walk three miles can't ya?"

They acknowledge the gentleman and make it to the two giant size kettles hot on the stove.

"Look at that, Choo Choo Train, its vegetable soup,"

Lucky Rails speaks softly and excitedly to him, and then gets directly in front of Choo Choo Train leading the way. Once they've got the bowls filled up, they go over to a table to sit with the others and they see there's bread and butter on the table, as well. No one is talking, but there is the sound of spoons splashing in the bowls of soup and the sound of cups going up and down on the table and their lips smacking.

A man sitting across from them raises his hand up in the air and says, "Get me a donut."

An elderly lady gets a tray filled with donuts and hands them out to everyone.

"That was good Choo Choo Train," Rhonda says as they are walking westward to the hobo jungle.

"That's right; I wish I could come again, Lucky Rails."

"Maybe there'll be some breakfast at the camp in the mornin'."

"Yeah…maybe."

~ 13 ~

The hobo jungle is near the railroad intersection where several lines meet, yet close enough to town where they can still look for work and find some supplies. There are some men in the jungle standing on higher ground, as though on a stage with lighted torches speaking out to all of them. The campfire is burning high and blazing.

"Congress put that Hawley-Smoot Tariff Act two years ago and has this kind of time we're in all over the world," the spokesman selected says to all of them gathered around.

"Because the tariff went up in price so high it's impossible to pay, and there's hundreds of economists against it, but President Hoover signed the bill into law, anyway," he continues.

"You see ... the other major trading nations raised their tariffs and that from the Hawley-Smoot ruin international trade, it's almost at a standstill," finishes the spokesman.

He turns away from the crowd and walks over to the others standing on higher ground as they all applaud. At that moment, another gentleman passes by him and speaks out:

"I'm here to spread the news too, and I'm here to tell you that I'm a Democrat. You all be sure to go vote and vote Roosevelt especially because the Republicans are still trying to have Hoover!"

The crowd is cheering him on clapping as loud as they can and screaming yaaeees...to pep rally for the event. However, just then, they come down from the higher ground and spill into the crowd of people who live in the hobo jungle to greet them and then get in their automobiles and go back to town. With the giant campfire still burning in the dark, the crowd of people are moving about in the dim light to resituate themselves and talk one to another.

"We're close enough now that I can see the jungle," says Lucky Rails.

"They got the fire burning hot," says Choo Choo Train. They're walking faster, since they have the jungle in their sight as they stride across the field with the railroad tracks along the side of them. It's a new experience for them whenever they get together with others in the same situation and when they steal aboard another train.

"My belly's really full since we got seconds on the bowl of soup, plus eaten all of that bread and butter," says Lucky Rails.

"I might get something to eat out here too if there's offerings," says Choo Choo Train.

"That's because you're a man, my stomachs already full and bloated," says Lucky Rails.

"We got some news to tell when we get there. Hewey Pewitt told us about the freight train coming out 'a Florida, it'll be headed straight to Lexington, Kentucky instead of stopping in Chattanooga," Choo Choo Train explains.

"That's right, he said they'll be switching tracks because his people talked to them down there," says Lucky Rails.

They've reached the hobo jungle and continue to walk in and stand before all of the ethnicities. The jungle broke the color barriers and has them sharing.

"I'll be Choo Choo Train Clarence Taylor, and this here is Lucky Rails Rhonda Smalls! We came in on this evening train; I'm in all the way from Florida after I left Virginia sometime ago this passing winter and now comes spring. Lucky Rails come up from Atlanta and we got news!"

"What news you got, Hobo?" shouts coming from the crowd of people that all of a sudden formed up around them.

"They're switching tracks at the Chattanooga Rails and bringing the cargo straight to you here in Lexington, Kentucky!"

"You'd best be givin' it to us straight on that and not be misleadin'!"

"That's right! Don't you come bad!"

The jungle is already excited from the ones that were there on the higher ground before Choo Choo Train and Lucky Rails got there. The people become joyous and fix smiles on their faces at the news to know a train will be coming directly with produce from the gardens of

Brian Douglas Beverly

Florida and other cargo. That gets them feeling better about how they will survive.

"You two can come sit with me and some other hoboes over here," comes a voice from off to the side.

~14~

Nine hoboes are sitting apart under a tree away from the big fire. Choo Choo Train and Lucky Rails follow the Hobo and sit with them. Coffee is offered from off the private fire they pitched for themselves.

"I'm Hobo Hard Steel Melvin Butterball. Hard Steel because I can jump down on a flat bed car from almost off the ruff of a boxcar, where I am on a ladder is pert~near~there, and it's as the train's movin' out, too," the man who walks them over to the other hoboes introduces himself. He is a very muscular man with all of the hair shaved off the top of his head and he stands five feet seven inches tall.

"I'm Slippery Paws Ted Winchell. I can slip my hands on the outer bars of the steel ladder and slip down with no feet touching the steps on the ladder from all the way at the top of it and only plant the first step." Slippery Paws grows his hair on his head down past his shoulders and wears a fifty gallon brim for his hat. And he has a thick mustache but he is without a beard.

"It's Caboose over here, and that's because I'm heavy like I am. Every time one of the other bo's see me, he'd tell me I'm the tail end of the train big like I am. So they got ta calling me Caboose. But ya know what? I can hop a train as good as a little guy can." Caboose is five feet nine inches tall and weighs three hundred pounds. He too has no hair on his head and like all of the other hoboes he has patches sewn over the top of the holes in his clothes.

Choo Choo Train and Lucky Rails are sitting down on a log drinking coffee. All of the hoboes sitting there tell their hobo name and the story behind it. A lot of the people there are Hoovervilles, Yeags and Tramps, very few bum because you don't ask for anything like that in the jungle.

"If 'n you two want somethin' to eat their's Mulligan stew, and we manage to scrounge-up pretty good," says Hard Steel Melvin Butterball.

"I don't mind if I do," says Choo Choo Train.

"I'm still full from the soup kitchen we found in town before we came out here," Lucky Rails replies.

Choo Choo Train leaves her sitting there and follows Hard Steel to the community soup.

"Say... You're a lady! You ain't no man!" Slippery Paws snatches the hat off Lucky Rails head after he sees her feminine figure shape-up in her clothes and he's staring her in the face.

"Give me my hat back," she keeps calm and wants him to cooperate.

He rises to his feet and pauses looking at Lucky Rails with her hat in his hands.

"Yeah. . . she sure is pretty." The other hoboes are interested and noticing her.

"Give it back to her," says Caboose.

"I'll let her have it alright," says Slippery Paws, and gives her the hat back.

"What was all of the excitement I saw when I was coming back?" Hard Steel asks.

"Look there, that's a lady," Slippery Paws answers.

"I know it is. I can see her. Plus Choo Choo Train standing here called her Rhonda when he said it's Lucky Rails," Hard Steel finishes.

Choo Choo Train Clarence Taylor says nothing and goes over to where she is and sits down, eating the Mulligan stew from out of a tin can using a wooden spoon.

"You said Florida's where you been?" Caboose asks.

"That's right, I was pick 'n oranges in Naples," says Choo Choo Train. "That's where I'm thinking to go except I'm get 'n with farms that has vegetables and livestock if I do," says Caboose.

"That'll be better than pick'n oranges. How's about somethin' leaving out of here?" Choo Choo Train asks.

"Their's a train pulling out of the yard at sun-up tomorrow morning headed to Cincinnati," says Caboose.

"That'll be good come tomorrow morning," Lucky Rails Rhonda

chimes in.

"You can use a shave, Choo Choo Train," says Caboose.

"I aint got no razor, or I would," says Choo Choo.

"After you finish eaten—I'll get you a razor," says Caboose.

Caboose takes some soap and water to a tree near by that has a mirror hanging from a nail, and their's a trash dumped next to it, he gets a whisky bottle from the trash and burst it against the tree. Then, he gives Choo Choo a large piece of it for shaving. Choo Choo Train manages to shave with it and only get's two cuts.

"Here comes five cars speedin' in," says Hard Steel.

The cars come to a crashing halt with their tires digging in the dirt. Ralf, Tom, and Billy get out of the leading car and walk into the Hobo jungle. The drivers in the other cars stay there, but the ones sitting on the passenger side get out with a loaded shot gun and post just ahead of the car.

"What do you bulls want with us out here?" asks one of the Hoovervilles.

"I'm gonna see what it is," says Hard Steel.

Slippery Paws follows walking fast and studying with him.

"Best we all stay here," Caboose suggests to the rest of them looking on."

"We're looking for the two that stole aboard the evening train that come-in tonight," Ralf shouts at the crowd of people that's gathered around him.

ONWARD

"They managed to escape out of a boxcar when I shut the door to hold them there, and I had my pistol too," Ralf continues.

"Their's two loose boards on the back wall. They managed to get out that way. If by chance they're here, I'm a wantin' you people ta fess up," Ralf finishes.

"That's right! You people fess up. I'm Bret Warner from out of the sheriff's department and their's a thief too. He's been get 'n around town these past two days and we got a positive description of him. And like those two," Ralf says.

"We believe back at the department they're here," shouts one of the deputies that's posted. Slippery Paws hurries back to where Choo Choo Train and Lucky Rails are standing with the other hoboes.

"Saaayy... That's gotta be you two, and they're looking for some yeag or tramp—who's thieving," Slippery Paws talks just above a whisper.

"Yep, that's us that stole aboard alright," replies Choo Choo Train.

"We gotta get out 'a here before they see us," Lucky Rails talks in a panicky way.

"Oh no! It's too late! They're all breaking through the barrier!" Slippery Paws sounds the alarm.

All of the hoboes are running away fast, and in no time, everyone in the jungle disperses.

The deputies and the bulls catch some of the hoboes and some of the others and take them to jail. Some of them fit the description of the thief. They want Choo Choo Train and Lucky Rails Rhonda as well.

58

Brian Douglas Beverly

~ 15 ~

In Toledo, Ohio there's a glass factory called Libbey Glass Company. In 1930, they were called the Libbey Glass-Owens-Ford Glass Company. As the market for fine cut glass diminished, Owens and Ford Glass dropped off from Libbey Glass. So now in 1932, the Libby Glass Company is making expensive machine-blown glass tumblers. The Purity Dairy Company purchases the tumblers for packaging their cottage cheese. They are reusable containers, and it's a success.

Chester Parks works at the Libbey Glass factory. He manages to take home enough money each week to maintain his family. His wife Lizzy Parks can prepare meals, whereas a lot of people can't, so they invite people over for dinner Wednesday and Sunday nights. Their kids, Phillip and Phyllis are grown and live on their own; they don't come for dinner on those nights because their parents are trying to help out by sparing some food to give away during these times of paralysis.

"My sister called the other night and said Rhonda's on her way here," says Lizzy.

"I remember you were saying something about that before."

"Yes she just now can get ta coming here but there's been some delay of the train. That's how she's coming is on a train," Lizzy adds.

Chester is done with work for the day, so he's home for the rest of the evening. He and Lizzy are sitting in the family room quiet and to themselves.

Brian Douglas Beverly

THE LIBBEY GLASS WORKS.
Sectional View.

~16~

Morning has come here in Lexington, Kentucky, and they've thrown in the county jail the ones they caught at the hobo jungle.

"Saaayy...bub did you see 'em get Slippery Paws or not?" asks one of the hoboes from his jail cell with his nose poking through the bars.

"No, they didn't catch him, but Hard Steel is three cells down from me," the hobo in the next cell answers from behind the bars.

"Just only Caboose and Slippery Paws got away," he continues.

"Ole yeah... and so did that Choo Choo Train Clarence Taylor and Lucky Rails Rhonda Smalls," finishes the first hobo.

The train bound for Cincinnati, Ohio on this morning's dawn is a very long freight train. It has all kinds of train cars attached, making it a slow and powerful tonnage of steel. From out of the weeds that's alongside of the tracks comes Slippery Paws dashing to the locomotive. It's as though he's first up to get aboard. He leaps into the open door of a boxcar, and Caboose gives him that much of a chance not to be seen.

Then he comes next and gets in a different boxcar the same way.

"We best go for that flat bed right there, Lucky Rails."

"Ok, Choo Choo Train."

They too have pitched themselves in the weeds not far off from the other two hoboes. They all spent the night hiding out in town until this morning. Now, Choo Choo Train and Lucky Rails is shooting out of the weeds. They're smacking small branches that gets leaves loose in the air and feeling the whip like tall weeds at their legs and tangling up at their ankles. Running faster and faster after the train as if they were in a race and quick out of the starter's block at the sound of the gun blasting off. First, Choo Choo Train reaches the flat bed train car. He throws his satchel on and then smacks his hands down on it and hops aboard.

"That's it, Lucky Rails! Now get up here like you just put your satchel! It's going plenty slow enough."

After Rhonda hops aboard, they get together in the middle of the flat bed and sit on the floor. Its eighty-one miles to Cincinnati, and the train plans to get there before noon. The train begins to pick up speed, moving steadily forward. The harsh wind coming against them makes the ride uncomfortable out in the open air. They've reached a curve and it rounds like the train's going to drive in a circle. The front brakeman is with the fireman shoveling coal into the furnace, but the big curve has slowed down the train enough, that so much coal is not needed for the time being.

"Let's take a break now Zebber," says the front brakeman.

"Fine by me."

They move back away from the furnace, and get all the way outside to stand on the iron stance that's to the hitch-up.

"Haaayy... now... Zebber, would you lookie there at them two," says the front brakeman.

"Yep, I see 'em, Lew."

"Hand me my double barrie here."

Zebber gets Lew his double barrel shot-gun that's leaning against the wall down by the furnace. They can see Choo Choo Train and Lucky Rails riding on the flat bed car because of the curve and that it's a lengthy train. Lew quickly climbs the ladder to the top of the first boxcar attached. He will go from one boxcar to the other until he reaches them on the flat bed.

Choo Choo and Lucky Rails didn't consider that they were too much out in the open and can be seen by the shacks.

"It's slow going around this curve, Lucky Rails," says Choo Choo Train.

"Yeah, we're taking a curve. Wow! Look up there, Choo Choo Train! That shack sees us and he's coming for us with a big gun!"

"That's right! I bet he don't see Slippery Paws or Caboose. He just only can see us because of this curve!"

"What are we gonna do, we can't go nowhere?!"

Lew's down a ladder, then comes back up the next boxcar.

"We straightened up now," says Lucky Rails, "But we're not going any faster!" she shouts.

"Hay, wait a minute, it's like we're up in the air," Choo Choo Train replies.

They come from the middle of the flat bed and go stand close to the edge, looking down.

"We're on a trestle now," says Lucky Rails.

"This is the Ohio River, and I can see the city. It's not really too far off from here," says Choo Choo Train.

Lucky Rails looking at him nodding her head can see the shack still coming. He is getting to the top of the boxcar attached to the flat bed.

"It looks like we're in the middle of the river now," says Choo Choo Train.

"He's almost here," says Lucky Rails.

~ 17 ~

"Here, give me your hand. We're gonna jump!" Choo Choo Train gets a hold of her hand. They throw the satchels off the train first. Just as Lew is aiming his double barrel shot gun, Choo Choo Train jumps off the train and brings Lucky Rails with him. They hit the water in an instant and fill up with it. They're wet and feel a kind of pressure that slows them down once they've plunged into the water and are sinking. They've stopped on the floor of the river and then like bubbles they begin to rise to the top, and then there's air.

"Lucky Rails! Lucky Rails!" cries Choo Choo Train.

His hands are splashing in the water, and he's looking all around for her. Lucky Rails breaks through the surface and gasps for air.

"Choo Choo Train!" she screams. "I'm behind ya! Turn around!"

"There you are, Lucky Rails!"

"Look up their," says Lucky Rails as they swim towards each other. They can see the shack watching them from high up in the air still standing on top of the boxcar.

"You two got away!" he shouts down at them pulling back his double barrel shot-gun, and starts walking back to the furnace as the train is slowly going over the trestle. The current takes them downriver a ways when they swim back for their satchels floating on top of the water. After they get their satchels, they manage to swim to the Cincinnati side of the river.

"We made it!" Lucky Rails says excitedly.

"Yes, we made it," Choo Choo Train tries to keep calm, but is just as excited as she is.

"I'm noticing what the river's like around here. It's like where I go fishing back home in Suffolk," he finishes.

"Oh... So it's like you been here before?" Lucky Rails Rhonda Smalls asks.

"Kind of, but not all together that," says Choo Choo Train Clarence Taylor.

"Now what, since we're all wet and without a train ride?"
she asks.

"Well... We can't stay here and build a fire because the matches are all wet. Let's start walking and see if their's a road near here, if there is, maybe someone driving by will pick us up on account of you being Lucky. I know one thing, that water's freezin' and so am I," finishes Choo Choo Train.

"We can't change our clothes either," says Lucky Rails Rhonda

Smalls.

"I know, our satchels are all wet," says Choo Choo Train Clarence Taylor.

They're walking away from the great Ohio River—through the woods. They find a road that leads to Cincinnati, and walk to town.

"I'm not going to call anyone and reverse the charges since we're this close," says Lucky Rails Rhonda Smalls.

"I'm not callin' anyone, either. Something could be in the mail for me when we get to Toledo though,' says Choo Choo Train.

"To go back to Suffolk and work at the depot you mean?"

"Yes, that would be great to hear from my mother—about that, because things seem to be the same all over, and I'm just want'n to get back to my people."

They get to the train station in Cincinnati, Ohio. Choo Choo Train has enough money to pay for the two train tickets to Toledo.

ONWARD

~ 18 ~

Once they arrive, Lucky Rails calls her Aunt Lizzy Parks. She and Chester come at once and drive the two of them to their house. "Is this where you live now?" Rhonda asks her aunt.

"Yes, we couldn't keep up with where we were, so we moved. It's better because of money," says Lizzy.

They all enter through the front door and spill into the living room. Rhonda gets clothes from out of their satchels and hangs them up on the bed room doors to dry. The clothes they're wearing are dry from walking and waiting for the train to Toledo from Cincinnati.

"I'm sure to get you on at the Glass factory, but you'll have to settle for the cut in pay like the rest of us. You said his name's Choo Choo Train?" Chester asks looking at Lucky Rails who is sitting down on the floor.

"I'm Clarence Taylor; Choo Choo Train's a nick name I picked-up in my travels."

ONWARD

"Yeah, and I got called Lucky Rails."

Clarence smiling goes over to where she is sitting on the floor and stands next to her.

"You can come with me on the weekends Rhonda, I'm cleaning office spaces downtown," says Aunt Lizzy.

Rhonda agrees to go to work with her aunt. Lizzy takes them into the kitchen and sits them at the supper table.

"It's ok to sit in those wooden chairs. I boiled this big ham today that's sitting here on top of the stove. And these are collard greens in that pot." She opens the oven door to show them what's in the oven. "Here is some macaroni and cheese in the oven," Lizzy finishes.

She puts a plate full of the food down on the table for each of them. And then she places a pan half filled with cornbread in the middle of the table along with some butter. Rhonda and Clarence will sleep in the spare rooms that used to be Phillip and Phyllis's rooms. Clarence explains he'll get a job in the city as soon as he's paid from working at the glass factory.

So far, everything is falling into place for Clarence Taylor. It's just what he had dreamed of—to go north and work at a factory and find a house on a street like this one with neighbors like Rhonda Smalls and her people.

Soon, he is able to move into a boarding house. He is steady at Libby's Glass factory, but finds out that his being optimistic is only so good. The 1929 Stock Market Crash had the same effects in Toledo as in Virginia.

He is sweeping the floors using a push broom and takes out the trash. Since cleaning is a big job at the factory, Clarence can get hired. There are times he wishes for a better position, but he knows he's lucky to be there and will do what's asked of him. He goes to see Rhonda one day out of each week and checks to see if any letter has come from his mother. Rhonda tells Clarence if a letter should arrive, she'll be sure and get it to him, but he can still stop in to see.

Rhonda Smalls is sitting on the sofa talking to Lizzy on this summer's morning, passing the time away. She is telling Lizzy about the times when she and Clarence were hopping trains and living like hoboes. She talks of when one hobo could no longer hang on to the ladder in Atlanta and fell to his death. And she tells about the time Clarence went into the bar and made the bet on drinking like he did. She talks about Hewey Pewitt, but the biggest story of all is about her and Clarence getting wet—they jumped into the Ohio River.

"I'll bet you were real scared get 'n on a train when it was still moving?"

"I sure was, Aunt Lizzy, every time I hopped a train it was different"

"You sure were brave, girl!"

"Aunt Lizzy, . . . I'm thinkin' about your mail delivery here. Clarence called his mother back and gave her this address instead of her having the one I gave him when we were in Tennessee."

"Sometimes mail gets delivered at our old address

because some people still have it, and it gets mixed up. And we've had to pick up at the post office before."

Their conversations go well into the afternoon, and they've moved from the living room to the kitchen to prepare the evening meal.

Clarence Taylor finishes working for the day and walks the two miles to where he is living. He stops at a fried chicken-to-go nearby and gets his dinner for the night. He puts it down on the table in his room along with a loaf of bread, but there isn't any butter. He washes in the bathroom at the end of the hallway like the rest of the tenants do.

After Clarence eats, he climbs into bed and falls asleep as soon as his head hits the pillow. The summertime here in Toledo, Ohio has lots of blooming flowers and tall green grass growing. And the wilderness that surrounds everything is full of pine trees with their scent filling the air.

Some more days have come and gone for Clarence Taylor, and he finds being in Toledo has him in a routine that feels limited. It goes against his nature.

~ 19 ~

Phillip Parks has come to his parents' house and sees his mother and Rhonda sitting in the living room talking as they do on weekdays.

"Hi Phillip, it's good to see you," Rhonda says.

"It's good to see you too. Hi mom." He walks across the room and sits comfortable in a big chair.

"Phillip, would you take me to your old house this afternoon to see if there's any mail in that mailbox? I want to check at the post office too," Rhonda asks.

"Yes, that'll be alright."

Most of the morning passes with conversations about the times Rhonda and her family came to Toledo to visit when she was a little girl. She is six years older than Phillip and can recall the baby he was then. Aunt Lizzy enjoys their company. She hardly feels the years of depression drag them down because Chester is still working.

Its two hours into the afternoon. Phillip and Rhonda drive down to the old house to see if there's any mail.

"You want to see if that letter came for Clarence Taylor, don't you?"

"Yes, that's right."

"It could be at our old address."

"We'll see."

When they arrive, Rhonda walks up to the mailbox. She sees there isn't any mail in it.

"Let's go check at the post office," she says closing the door after she get's back into the car.

Phillip drives her to the post office and Rhonda goes in to ask the postmaster at the counter. He finds a small stack of letters for Lizzy and Chester Parks. Rhonda comes out with them and is looking the envelopes over as she walks back to the car.

"Another one to Lizzy and Chester, and here's one to Phyllis, Clarence Taylor. Ole my Goodness, it's been here at the post office all this time!"

"Come on, get in!" Phillip shouts coaxing her back into the car as she is walking slowly.

"This is a letter to Clarence from his mother. It's what I was after. Drive to the factory so I can give it to him, that's where he is right now."

Phillip can see the excitement in Rhonda's face and is driving as fast as he can without going too much over the speed limit.

"We'll make the next turn, and then it'll be up the street a little ways," says Phillip. Just when he says that, the right front tire goes flat, and he has to pull over to get the spare. They get out of the car and stand on the sidewalk looking at the tire. Rhonda has Clarence's letter in her hand and opens it to read it.

"Listen Phillip, I can walk there by the time you change the tire. Can you come get me at the factory?"

"Yes," he answers.

She's walking fast and takes off running at top speed. As she gets to the factory, she sees Clarence outside, sweeping. He is gripping the big push broom with both hands and there's a flat head shovel lying on the ground for sweep up the piles.

"Hay, Choo Choo Train! Choo Choo Train! You can go home now!"

He turns to Lucky Rails's voice calling to him faintly coming from behind.

"Lucky Rails!" he shouts when he sees her waving the letter in the air and running towards him.

"Your letter came. Mr. Foster got the contract! You can go back home now!"

Choo Choo Train Clarence Taylor lets the broom handle drop from his hands and runs to Lucky Rails. When he gets to her he grabs her up in his arms and the both of them have tears of joy.